AXEL SCHEFFL

Mother Goose's Action Rhymes

With stories by Alison Green

MACMILLAN CHILDREN'S BOOKS

First published 2006 in *Mother Goose's Nursery Rhymes* by Macmillan Children's Books
This collection published 2009 by Macmillan Children's Books
a division of Macmillan Publishers Limited
20 New Wharf Road, London N1 9RR
Basingstoke and Oxford
Associated companies throughout the world
www.panmacmillan.com

ISBN: 978-0-230-01814-3

Text copyright © Macmillan Children's Books 2006, 2009
Illustrations copyright © Axel Scheffler 2006, 2009
The right of Axel Scheffler to be identified as the
Illustrator of this work has been asserted by him in accordance
with the Copyright Designs and Patents Act 1988.

1 3 5 7 9 8 6 4 2

A CIP catalogue record for this book is available from the British Library.

Printed in Belgium

CONTENTS

One fine spring day a mother goose laid three eggs. When her goslings hatched out she called them Boo, Lucy and Small. Boo was the first to hatch out – he was the biggest and noisiest. Next came Lucy, who had the flappiest wings. Last of all was little Small, the quietest, dreamiest gosling.

Mother Goose was very proud of her little family. She taught them how to swim and how to fly, how to waddle after her in a nice tidy line, and all of the other important things that goslings have to know. There was a lot for them to learn, but luckily there was always time for playing too.

All three were very busy little goslings, and they never sat still if they could help it. Boo, Lucy and Small much preferred having swimming races or chasing each other along the sunny riverbank. But what the goslings liked best was when Mother Goose would tell them nursery rhymes.

She knew all sorts of rhymes: noisy ones and quiet ones, rhymes for playtime, and even rhymes with actions. So when the goslings were too full of bounce to concentrate, Mother Goose would tell them a rhyme and they all joined in with the actions. They loved clapping along to "Pat-a-cake" and dancing around in a circle to "Ring-a-ring o' Roses" – Boo liked falling down at the end the best!

It wasn't long before other mother geese started to tell the rhymes to their own goslings. Now all the very best action rhymes have been gathered together in this book for you and your family to join in with, too.

Pat-a-cake

Clap along with the rhyme!

Pat-a-cake, pat-a-cake, baker's man,
Bake me a cake as fast as you can;
Pat it and prick it, and mark it with B,
Put it in the oven for baby and me.

Pease Porridge

This is another good rhyme to clap along to.

Pease porridge hot,
Pease porridge cold,
Pease porridge in the pot
Nine days old.

Some like it hot,
Some like it cold,
Some like it in the pot
Nine days old.

I'm a Little Teapot

Join in with the actions!

I'm a little teapot, short and stout;

Here's my handle, here's my spout.

> *Put one hand on your hip, and hold the other out like the spout of a teapot.*

When I see the teacups, hear me shout,

"Tip me up and pour me out."

> *Lean over towards your "spout" arm, as if you're pouring out tea.*

T he goslings were having a sleepy morning.

"Time to get up!" called Mother Goose. "Breakfast time!"

"I'm tired, Mummy," said Lucy.

"So am I," said Small.

"So am I," said Boo.

"Oh dear," said Mother Goose. "We must have waddled too far yesterday. I've got an idea. Let's wait a bit and watch the trains go by before we have breakfast."

The goslings loved watching the trains. After they'd watched five trains go by Mother Goose said, "Shall we be a train now, chugging all the way down to the river? I'll be the engine, and you be the carriages following behind me."

"Can I say, 'Off we go'?" asked Lucy.

"Yes, you can," said Mother Goose. "And Boo and Small can make all the train noises."

So Lucy shouted, "One, two, three – off we go!" and Boo and Small shouted, "Chug-chug!" and "Toot-toot!" all the way to the river.

Down by the Station

Down by the station
Early in the morning,
See the little puffer trains
All in a row.
    See the engine driver
    Turn the little handle.
    Chug-chug,
    Toot-toot,
Off we go.

Chook, Chook, Chook

Chook, chook, chook, chook, chook,
Good morning, Mrs Hen.
How many chickens have you got?
Madam, I've got ten.
Four of them are yellow,
And four of them are brown,
And two of them are speckled red,
The nicest in the town.

Ring-a-ring o' Roses

All hold hands and skip round in a ring.
On the last line, all sit down on the ground.

Ring-a-ring o' roses,

A pocket full of posies.

A-tishoo! A-tishoo!

We all fall down.

T he goslings had been playing ring o' roses all morning. They were all rather dizzy.

"Ring-a-ring-a-ring-a-ring-a-ring," sang Small, spinning round in circles. Then he fell down on his bottom with a bump.

Lucy and Boo did the same, and soon they were all lying in a heap, giggling.

"Oh dear," said Mother Goose. "This doesn't look like the best time to start your flying lessons."

"We can do flying tomorrow – hic!" said Lucy. She'd laughed so much she'd got hiccups.

"Sing us another rhyme, Mummy," said Small.

"Very well," sighed Mother Goose. "I'll sing you one where you have to wave your wings about. At least that will make them strong for flying. It's called *Incey Wincey Spider* . . ."

Incey Wincey Spider

Join in the actions!

Incey wincey spider
Climbing up the spout;

*Use all your fingers to show
how the spider climbs up.*

Down came the rain
And washed the spider out:

*Wriggle your fingers down
to show the rain.*

Out came the sun
And dried up all the rain;

*Sweep your hands up and
bring them out and down.*

Incey wincey spider
Climbing up again.

*Do the same as for the
first verse.*

Ride a Cock-horse

Ride a cock-horse to Banbury Cross,
To see a fine lady upon a white horse;
Rings on her fingers and bells on her toes,
And she shall have music wherever she goes.

Row, Row, Row Your Boat

Row, row, row your boat
Gently down the stream.
Merrily, merrily, merrily, merrily,
Life is but a dream.

T he goslings were having a swimming lesson.

"I like that rhyme," sighed Small. "I wish we had a boat to row. It would be much easier than swimming."

"I know some different words to that rhyme," said Boo. "They go like this," and he sang:

"Row, row, row your boat,
Gently down the stream.
If you see a crocodile,
Don't forget to scream!"

"Crocodile!" screamed Small. He scrambled out of the water as fast as he could, and wouldn't come back in.

"Come on, Small," called Mother Goose. "There aren't any crocodiles in this river."

But Small wouldn't come back until Mother Goose waddled out and gave him a cuddle.

"Let's just sing my words in future, shall we?" she said.

This Little Pig

*Starting with the big toe, pretend each of your gosling's toes is
a little pig. On the last line, tickle her under the foot.*

This little pig went to market,

This little pig stayed at home,

This little pig had roast beef,

This little pig had none,

And this little pig cried, Wee-wee-wee-wee-wee,

    All the way home.

Hickety, Pickety, My Black Hen

Hickety, pickety, my black hen,

She lays eggs for gentlemen;

Gentlemen come every day

To see what my black hen doth lay.

Sometimes nine and sometimes ten,

Hickety, pickety, my black hen.

Here We Go Round the Mulberry Bush

Here we go round the mulberry bush,
The mulberry bush, the mulberry bush,
Here we go round the mulberry bush,
On a cold and frosty morning.

This is the way we wash our hands,
Wash our hands, wash our hands,
This is the way we wash our hands,
On a cold and frosty morning.

This is the way we wash our clothes,
Wash our clothes, wash our clothes,
This is the way we wash our clothes,
On a cold and frosty morning.

"**T**his is the way we fish for weed, fish for weed, fish for weed," sang Lucy, dunking her head in the water. She came up again a moment later, coughing and spluttering.

"Eat first, dear," said Mother Goose, "and then sing. You can't do both at once."

"I can if I practise," said Lucy.

"I don't think so, dear," said Mother Goose, but it was too late. Lucy had already ducked under the water, and bubbles were rising up where she was singing.

A few seconds later she was up again, coughing so hard she went bright red in the beak.

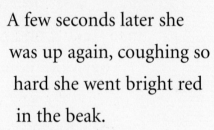

"A bit of weed went down the wrong way," she gasped.

"Oh, I see," said Mother Goose. "I thought it was the singing that made you cough."

"Oh, no," said Lucy, and she sang, "This is the way we cough up weed, cough up weed, cough up weed –"

"Those aren't the nicest words to sing, dear," said Mother Goose. "How about I sing you an eating song while you have your lunch? It's called *Polly Put the Kettle On* . . ."

Polly Put the Kettle On

Polly put the kettle on,
Polly put the kettle on,
Polly put the kettle on,
We'll all have tea.

Sukey take it off again,
Sukey take it off again,
Sukey take it off again,
They've all gone away.

Blow the fire and make the toast,
Put the muffins on to roast,
Who is going to eat the most?
We'll all have tea.

Round and Round the Garden

Round and round the garden
Like a teddy bear;
Run your finger round your gosling's palm.

One step, two step,
"Jump" your fingers up his arm.

Tickly under there!
Tickle him under his arm.

This Is the Way the Ladies Ride

Cross your legs and sit your gosling over your top ankle, facing you.
Hold hands tightly, and jump her up and down to the rhyme. On the
last line, let her slip down gently over your toes to the ground.

This is the way the ladies ride,

Trippety-trip, trippety-trip;

This is the way the gentlemen ride,

A-gallop-a-trot, a-gallop-a-trot;

This is the way the farmers ride,

Jiggety-jog, jiggety-jog;

And when they come to a hedge – they jump over!

And when they come to a slippery place – they

    scramble, scramble,

        Tumble-down Dick!

Two Little Dicky Birds

Join in the actions! Use your two
index fingers to be Peter and Paul.

Two little dicky birds,

Sitting on a wall;

One named Peter,

The other named Paul

    Waggle each finger in turn.

Fly away, Peter!

    Put "Peter" behind your back.

Fly away, Paul!

    Put "Paul" behind your back.

Come back, Peter!

Come back, Paul!

    Bring each finger back
    in front of you.

**T**wo sparrows were hopping around in the brambles. Boo wanted to say hello, so he ran up to one of them, flapping his wings.

"Hello, birdie!" he shouted, but the sparrow flew away. So he ran up to the other sparrow. "Hello, other birdie!" he shouted, but that sparrow flew away, too.

"I don't think they heard me, Mummy," he said, sadly.

"You frightened them off," said Mother Goose. "You have to be quiet and gentle with birdies, and even then they sometimes fly away. They're very timid."

"What's timid?" asked Boo.

"It means they get frightened easily," said Mother Goose.

"I'm not timid, am I?" said Boo.

"Not very, dear, no," said Mother Goose.

Boo looked sad. "I was just being friendly," he said.

"I know you were," said Mother Goose. "But birdies still get scared, just like in this rhyme . . ."

Once I Saw a Little Bird

Once I saw a little bird
    Come hop, hop, hop,
And I cried, "Little bird,
    Will you stop, stop, stop?"

I was going to the window
    To say, "How do you do?"
But he shook his little tail
    And away he flew.

Rub-a-dub-dub

Rub-a-dub-dub,
Three men in a tub,
And who do you think they be?
The butcher, the baker,
The candlestick-maker,
Turn 'em out, knaves all three.

One, Two, Three, Four, Five

One, two, three, four, five,

Once I caught a fish alive,

Six, seven, eight, nine, ten,

Then I let it go again.

Why did you let it go?

Because it bit my finger so.

Which finger did it bite?

This little finger on the right.

If All the Seas Were One Sea

If all the seas were one sea,

What a *great* sea that would be!

If all the trees were one tree,

What a *great* tree that would be!

And if all the axes were one axe,

What a *great* axe that would be!

And if all the men were one man,

What a *great* man that would be!

And if the *great* man took the *great* axe,

And cut down the *great* tree,

And let it fall into the *great* sea,

What a splish-splash that would be!

"If all the geese were one goose," said Boo, "that would be a really ginormous huge goose, wouldn't it?"

"Yes," said Mother Goose.

"When he waddled the ground would shake," said Lucy.

"That's right," said Mother Goose.

"And when he said, 'Honk!' it would sound like a trumpet," said Boo.

"It would," said Mother Goose.

"And when he flapped his wings, all the trees would fall down," said Lucy.

"That would be scary," said Mother Goose.

"I think geese are best being normal size," said Small.

"I think so, too," said Mother Goose.

Index of First Lines